The Adventures of the Itty Bitty Spider and the Itty Bitty Mouse

Kimberly P. Johnson
Illustrated by Landa Smith

Visit the author at:
www.simplycreativeworks.com

Pentland Press, Inc.
England • USA • Scotland

Other works by the author:

The Adventures of the Itty Bitty Frog
The Adventures of the Itty Bitty Bunny

PUBLISHED BY PENTLAND PRESS, INC.
5122 Bur Oak Circle, Raleigh, North Carolina 27612
United States of America
(919)782-0281

ISBN: 1-57197-236-6
Library of Congress Catalog Card Number 00-133645

Printed in China

A Few Words About Kimberly Johnson and Her Work . . .

Children will find delight in the journey of the spider and the mouse. This story is entertaining and exciting! It is sensitively illustrated with an important and valuable moral lesson. Young children can certainly become knowledgeable of the precious trait of honesty through the words of this story. This book should be among the most popular children's books and take its place with books that endure.

Felton A. Thomas, Ed. D.
Department of Elementary Education
School of Education
Fayetteville State University

There is no greater delight than reading a really good book to children. I read to all three of my children and it was the highlight of our day as we settled into our newest book. Some books they wanted to hear over and over. The measure of a good book was when I enjoyed the book as much as they did.

Kim Johnson's **The Adventures of the Itty Bitty Spider and the Itty Bitty Mouse** is truly one those books that both children and adults will enjoy reading over and over. Kim has captured a spirit of light-heartedness with delightful poetry, while subtly teaching lessons that parents will embrace.

Senator Ellie Kinnaird
The General Assembly of North Carolina

Not only great joy but a marvelous opportunity to recognize and commend Kimberly Johnson has come my way . . . . As she writes stories for growing children, she reveals an affection for the world of nature. . . . The biography of Kimberly Johnson would reveal a spiritual foundation upon which she has built her life. Her work encourages children to demonstrate love, character and hope. Probing minds of children will meet creative expression in its purest form!

Mary Lois Staton
Professor Emeritus
East Carolina University

This book is dedicated to my family
and to all who believe in and love my "itty bitty" characters.

Jeff - Thank you for your unconditional love and support.
Each day, you teach me greater lessons about life. You are my inspiration!!

Dr. Thomas, Dr. Staton, and Senator Kinnaird - Your words are so kind.

Sherron Hornaday, Dulcina Fike, and Mary Lou Mackintosh - Thank you for sharing your wisdom!

Landa Smith - Thanks for your hard work and dedication. We did it again!

"FOR UNTO WHOM MUCH IS GIVEN, MUCH IS ALSO REQUIRED"

*BELIEVE IN YOURSELF,
AND WONDERFUL THINGS WILL HAPPEN!*

In the itty bitty corner of an itty bitty house,
lived an itty bitty spider and an itty bitty mouse.

"I am bored," said the spider. "Me, too," said the mouse. "Come on, then. Let's get out of this house."

So, they walked past the bird and the calico cat.

3

They walked past the dog that was asleep on the mat.

4

They walked past Mom, and they walked past Dad.

5

6   They walked past the ball that the baby had.

When they got outside into the bright, bright sun, the mouse said to the spider, "That sure was fun!

Let's go to the store on the corner of the street and maybe we can buy something good to eat."

So, they walked past the snake that was lying in the grass.

8

They walked past the school and the children in the class.

10   They walked past Betty Beetle who was talking to a bee.

They walked past Susie Squirrel who was playing in her tree.

When they got to the store on the corner of the street,
the spider said, "Let's take our money and buy something to eat."

12

They took out the money that they had saved for weeks,
that is when they saw the chipmunk filling up his cheeks.

13

The itty bitty spider said, "You cannot take food without paying!"

The chipmunk replied,"Listen to me spider, hear what I am saying."

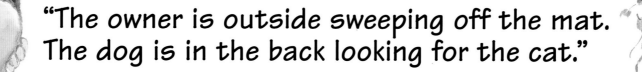

"The owner is outside sweeping off the mat.
The dog is in the back looking for the cat."

"There is no one to see me, no one to tell.
There is no one to accuse me or to send me to jail."

16

The mouse said, "Stealing is wrong, and it is also a crime.
If you steal just once, you will steal all the time.

It is not worth the risk. It is not worth the shame.
It is not worth the label that is placed on your name."

"Come on, chipmunk, put those things back
Don't do crime. Stay on the right track."

CANDY

"Yes, you are right," said the chipmunk with shame.
"It is all my fault. There is no one to blame."

18

"Thanks for telling me the right thing to do.
I will never steal again, and I owe it to you!"

"No," said the itty bitty mouse, "YOU chose to do right.
We helped you see the choices. We helped you see the light."

The chipmunk smiled. "I will come back when I have money to spend."
The spider looked up with a big, wide grin.
"Please don't leave. Come back here, my friend."

"How can I be your friend?" asked the chipmunk.
"You saw what I was going to take."
"It's alright," said the mouse. "You made a mistake."

"We all do things that sometimes we should not do, but if we are wise enough to fix them, then we will always shine through."

To show the chipmunk that they really did care, the spider and the mouse decided to share.

The friends left the store with a goodie and a treat.
They all waved good-bye until again they would meet.

Then the itty bitty spider and the itty bitty mouse
decided to go back home to their itty bitty house.

So, they walked past Susie Squirrel
who was sitting near her tree.

They walked past Betty Beetle
who was talking to a bee.

Bee Sweet
Honey

They walked past the school and the children in the class.

24

They walked past the snake that was lying in the grass.

They walked past the ball that the baby had.
They walked past Mom, and they walked past Dad.

They walked past the dog that was asleep on the mat.
They walked past the bird and the calico cat.

26

When they made it safely home to their itty bitty house,
the mouse thanked the spider and the spider thanked the mouse.

The End